D1030669

THE DRAGON ABC HUNT

THE DRAGON ABC HUNT
WRITTEN AND ILLUSTRATED BY
LOREEN LEEDY
HOLIDAY HOUSE · NEW YORK

For my parents, GRACE AND JIM

Library of Congress Cataloging-in-Publication Data

The dragon ABC hunt.

Summary: Ten little dragons try to find an object for each letter of the alphabet.
[1. Dragons—Fiction. 2. Alphabet. 3. Stories in rhyme] I. Title.
PZ8.3.L4995Dr 1986 [E] 85-21907
ISBN 0-8234-0596-6

Ten little dragons are bored one day
And very grumpy, too.
Ma knows a game they all can play,
She tells them what to do.

"Here's a list of things to find,
Words from *A* to *Z*,
Search up and down, above, behind,
Bring treasures back to me!"

Aa

Bb

ball

Cc

cat

Dd
dog

Ee

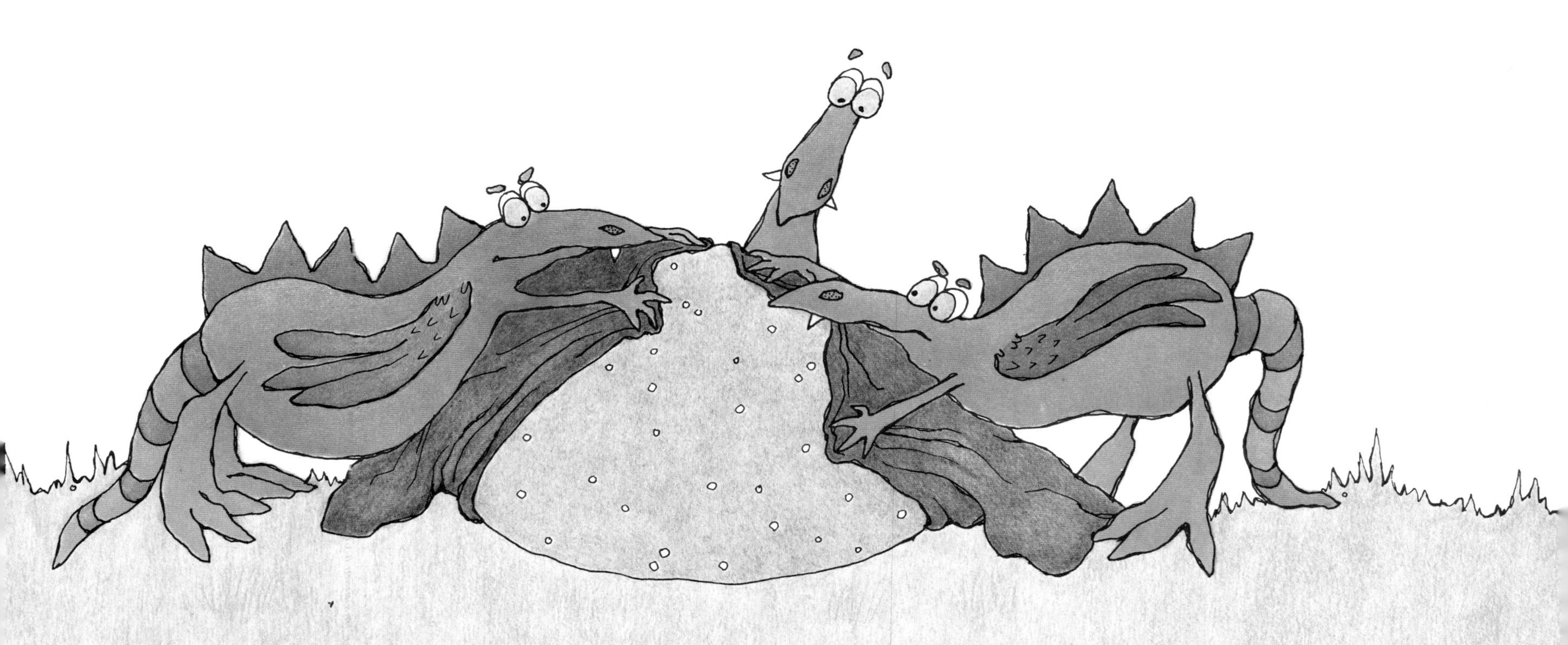

egg

Ff

Gg

Hh
hat

I i

iguana

Jj
jewel

Kk
kite

Ll

lollipop

Mm
mask

Nn
nest

Oo
ostrich

pillow

Qq
queen

Rr
rock

Ss

sock

turtle

Uu

umbrella

violin

Ww

watermelon

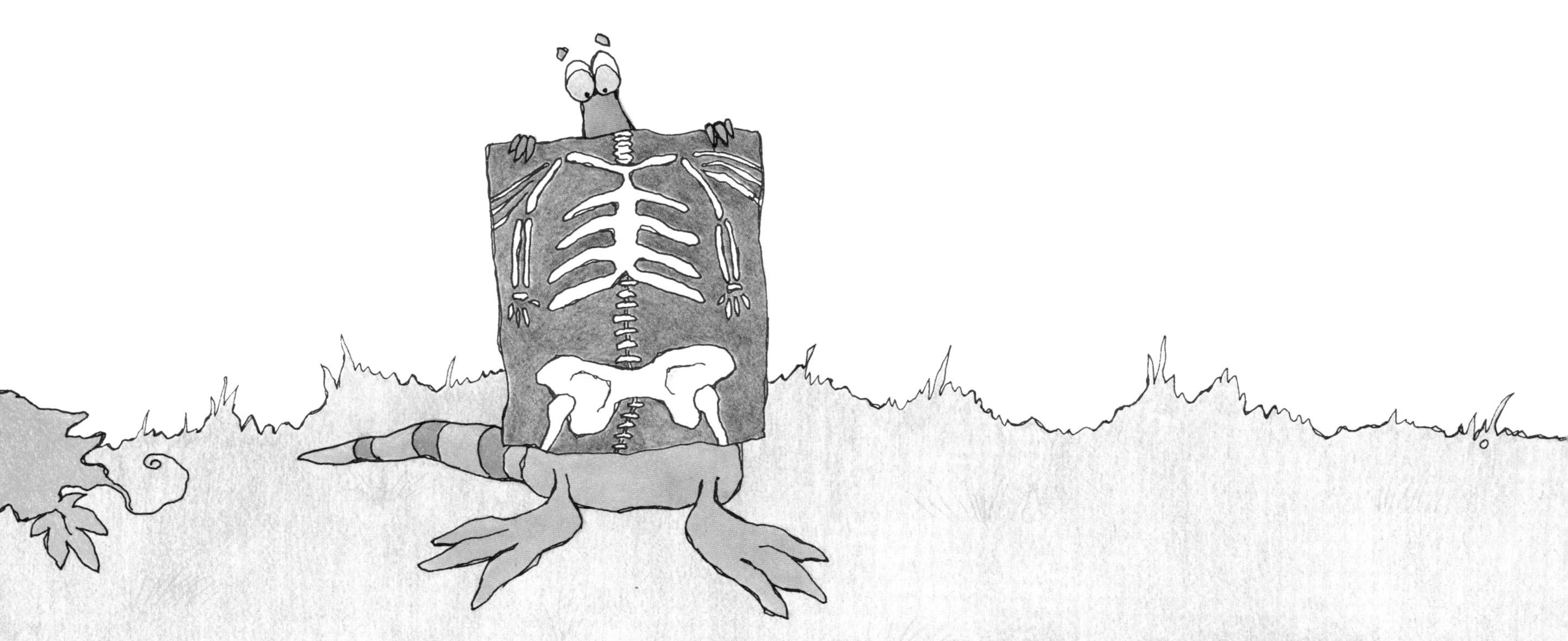

x-ray

Y y
yo-yo

Zz
zebra

Ten little dragons giggle and run,
Happy as they sing,
"Scavenger hunts are lots of fun!
We found everything!"

Ma Dragon says, “We’re almost done . . .
Get in order, please!”
The dragons line up one by one
And say their *ABC*’s.

Aa Bb Cc Dd Ee Ff
Gg Hh Ii Jj Kk Ll Mm
Nn Oo Pp Qq Rr Ss Tt
Uu Vv Ww Xx Yy Zz